Other Books About Inge

TIKHON

ILSE-MARGRET VOGEL

Pictures by the author

✳ ✳ ✳

HARPER & ROW, PUBLISHERS

For my Howard-husband . . . .

... but this copy is for ....,
a little friend of Mary.
With best wishes and love
Else-Margret Vogel
Bengall, Dec. 1991

TIKHON

Designed by Joyce Hopkins
1   2   3   4   5   6   7   8   9   10

FIRST EDITION

Library of Congress Cataloging in Publication Data
Vogel, Ilse-Margret.
  Tikhon.

  Summary: Tikhon, a Russian soldier trapped without
identification papers in post-World War I Germany,
becomes a unique and much-loved companion to young Inge
when her parents harbor him in their basement.
  [1. Friendship—Fiction.   2. World War, 1914–1918—
Refugees.   3. Germany—Fiction]   I. Title.
PZ7.V867Ti 1984   [Fic]   83-48443
ISBN 0-06-026328-8
ISBN 0-06-026329-6 (lib. bdg.)

CONTENTS

Foreword

This story takes place in a defeated Germany shortly after the end of World War I. Order had not yet returned to a country that had suffered great losses and hardship. There was hunger and poverty, and jobs were scarce. Although Russia was one of the victors in this war, some Russian soldiers, who had been prisoners of war, were still in Germany. With nobody to issue discharge papers, they found themselves without any official identification. As "illegal aliens" they were in danger of being picked up by the German police and held in prison until their identity was cleared. Bewildered and afraid in a country whose language they did not speak, whose very alphabet they could not read, they wandered from town to town and from village to village looking for odd jobs to earn enough money to return home to their beloved "Mother Russia." They depended entirely on the generosity and helpfulness of their former enemies, the German people. They were sometimes abused by their employers, who took advantage of their precarious situation. But even when they were treated kindly, they did not dare stay long in one place for fear they might come to the attention of the German police.

Such a person is our Tikhon.

TIKHON

Chapter One

I woke up happy. It was Saturday, and Papa had
come home the night before after a week of ab-
sence. I had not seen him because he had arrived
after my bedtime.

I was looking forward to the weekend with Papa.
Since my twin sister had died, I was an only child
and often felt lonely during the week; especially
when Dodo, my grandmother, was away visiting
my Uncle Max. There were no children of my age

in the neighborhood, and I wasn't even allowed to go to school. We lived on the outskirts of a small town, and Mother didn't let me take the long walk to school because she worried.

"Never talk to strangers," Mother always told me. "Never accept a chocolate or candy from a stranger."

The war was over and hard times had fallen on Germany. Stories of crimes filled the newspapers. There were even rumors, Mother said, that terrible men abducted children and *slaughtered* them.

"Doesn't one slaughter only animals?" I asked.

"That's it," Mother said, "that's it. There are rumors of madmen who kill children and mix their meat with beef."

I had to laugh. "That can't be true, Mama," I said. "*Nobody* would want to eat that."

Mother threw her arms around me and held me tight. "Darling, you must be careful. Promise me!"

I promised, and from that day on I always made a little curtsy when I saw a man coming toward me on the road. I would start my curtsy when the man was still far away, repeating it every few steps

4

till I had passed him. If this man has bad intentions, I told myself, he will be charmed by my politeness and not dare abduct me, much less *slaughter* me. Should he offer a chocolate, well . . . I would have to turn it down politely. "Oh no, thank you," I would have to say. "I'm too full of chocolates today. I've eaten about a pound already." However, nobody ever offered me any chocolate. Still, my curtsying must have helped: I was never abducted either.

I promised Mother to be careful, but she kept on worrying just the same. The moment I was out of her sight, she worried.

Therefore Mr. Keller was hired to teach me at home. He came every day on his bicycle, his coat flapping behind him like the wings of a huge bird. I liked Mr. Keller, though he was a man of many faces: one day happy, the next day sad. His nose, however, was always red, which made him look funny even on his sad days. Once or twice a month Mr. Keller would show up very late or, sometimes, not at all. That too caused Mother to worry. "He made himself sick again," she would say. "What do you mean, *made* himself sick?" I would ask. Mother would only shake her head and frown.

But today was Saturday and Mr. Keller would not come. My clock struck seven. Darkness was slowly giving way to the gray light of morning, but I knew it would still be a long time before Papa woke up. So I decided to watch the sun rise behind the Zobten Mountain. This time of year the big lump of the mountain stood sharp and clear against the glowing sky, and for a few minutes it would seem as if the mountain itself were sending out rays of sunlight. I climbed out of bed and went to the window facing east. There was only a pale shimmer of yellow at the horizon.

Suddenly I heard a sound; faint and quivering; it didn't sound like anything I had ever heard before. I opened the window and the sound got clearer, changing into a slow and haunting melody.

I dressed quickly, then tiptoed downstairs and out the back door. There I heard the music again. Nobody was in sight; the music, however, went on. I had taken a few steps when I heard a knock at the glass pane of the cellar window. I could not see clearly through the reflecting glass, but something moved behind it. I knelt down and suddenly came face to face with another face. A huge face with wide cheekbones and small bright-blue eyes under bushy blond eyebrows. I stepped back hastily and curtsied, even though there was a window between us. What was a stranger doing in our basement? He opened the window slowly, stretched out a huge hand and said something I could not understand. I shook my head.

"I Tikhon," he said, pointing to himself. Then he extended his hand again, and he seemed so friendly that I could not help but trust him. Carefully I went closer and took his hand.

"Tikhon," he said again.

I tried to repeat his name but could not. There was a sound in the middle of the word I had never heard before: It rattled in his throat like a snore. Tikhon laughed.

I pointed to myself and said, "Inge."

Tikhon nodded, frowned and repeated, "Jinge."

7

"No, no," I said, "IN-ge."

He tried once more and slowly, very slowly, said, "Jinge" again.

When he saw me shake my head and laugh, he shrugged and gave a vague gesture with his hand.

For a while we just looked at each other; then Tikhon dug his hand into the pocket of his fur-lined vest, pulled out something and put it to his mouth. I could not see what it was—but instantly I heard the music again. Tikhon's huge hands moved to and fro in front of his mouth. *They* seemed to make the music. I leaned forward, trying to see better. Tikhon stopped and handed me something. "Armonica," he said.

I was looking at a rectangular piece of metal with rows of small holes on each side, when Tikhon suddenly exclaimed: "Sun! Look sun!"

And there it was! I had forgotten about the sunrise. We both looked in silence as the sun came up over the top of the Zobten Mountain.

"Sun!" Tikhon repeated, awe in his voice. "Sun come from . . . I come from . . . east . . . ome . . . far."

I didn't know what he meant, but I liked watching the sun and watching Tikhon watch the sun. After the sun had cleared the mountain completely, Tikhon broke the silence.

"My ome—far avay—a mountain, too."

I was bewildered; what did he mean?

"You live in the mountains?" I asked.

"No," he replied, "not in mountains. Only—" and he held up his right fist with just the index finger raised.

"Oh," I said, "just *one* mountain?"

Tikhon nodded eagerly. "One mountain—far avay—like dis," and he pointed to the Zobten.

Then, all at once, he turned and walked into the darkness of the cellar. "Vait," he called over his shoulder, and soon he was back at the window, beckoning me to come closer.

"Take," he said, stretching his hands through the window and putting something into my hands. It was hard, and flat on the bottom and half round on top, with a pretty pattern of irregular black and yellow squares. Suddenly something moved inside. I was so startled I dropped it on the grassy ground.

10

"No! No!" Tikhon cried. "You no fear!" Just then a little head peeked out at one end and the whole thing moved a bit.

"Good . . . my Manya no urt," said Tikhon. "Dis Manya, my shieldfrog."

I had never seen or heard of a shieldfrog and wanted to take a closer look, but I heard Papa calling me. I gave Manya back to Tikhon and ran into the house. Breathless, I arrived in Papa's arms.

"It has been a long time," he said.

"Yes," I said. "Did you bring me a present?"

"No," Papa smiled, "but I have a surprise for you. I brought—"

"Tikhon?" I asked.

"How did you know?" asked Papa.

"We watched the sunrise together," I answered, "and Tikhon played his armonica—"

"Harmonica," Papa corrected.

"—and he showed me his shieldfrog."

"His turtle," said Papa, laughing. "Yes, Tikhon loves his harmonica and his turtle."

"Who is Tikhon?" I wanted to know. "And why is he in our cellar?"

11

"That is a long story," Papa replied. "It has to do with ugly things like wars and revolutions."

"You brought Tikhon to live with us?" I asked.

Papa sighed. "Not really; but Tikhon needs help. He needs money to pay his way home to Russia."

"Is Russia in the east?" I asked. "And is it far awa?"

Papa nodded. "We will help Tikhon by letting him help us. He will stay for a few weeks."

"Help with what?" I asked.

"Well, he is willing to do some garden work, although he is a cabinetmaker. A very fine one, I understand."

"Papa, where did you find Tikhon?" I asked. Did he come to you for help?"

"No, Inge, Tikhon would not dare do that. You see, his existence in Germany is not quite legal, which is not really his fault. He has no official papers, and he is afraid he would be put in prison or a work camp if the police found him. So he has to move from place to place working wherever he can find a job. He stayed with a colleague of mine for a couple of months doing all kinds of repairs

12

in the house. But now my colleague felt Tikhon should move on, and he asked me if we wouldn't have some use for him." Papa stopped.

I had listened spellbound. "Go on," I urged, "go on."

"That's all. More I don't know about Tikhon. It's difficult to find out more, because Tikhon knows only a few German words and hardly anybody in this country speaks Russian."

"I'll teach him German," I declared. "And maybe I'll learn a little Russian from him. Then we will understand each other."

Papa smiled. "Well," he said, "a sign language might be easier for both of you."

Chapter Two

After breakfast I hurried outdoors, hoping to see Tikhon. I found him behind the house, leaning over the fence of our vegetable garden.

"Hello," I said, stepping close to him.

"Allo," he responded.

"You must say 'Hel-lo,' Tikhon," I told him, speaking slowly and separating the word carefully.

"Can't," he said.

14

"But it is easy," I said, "listen." And I repeated "Hel-lo" very slowly.

Tikhon shook his head. "No easy," he said. "Russian no ave no—" and with great effort he pressed breath out of his mouth.

I laughed, but did not want to give up. "Hel-lo," I said again and again. "Please, Tikhon, try!"

He didn't. Instead he grinned, blinked at me and said, "You say 'Tikhon.'"

Well, there I was. Stuck. Because there was no way I could make it sound the way he said it. The k in the center of his name came out a clear k when I said it. But in Tikhon's mouth it was a rasping sound coming from the depths of his throat. "Say it," Tikhon insisted. I tried and tried till we both laughed and laughed and could not stop laughing. Exhausted from so much laughing, I started to lean against a garden fence post.

"Don't," warned Tikhon. He bent down and showed me that the post had rotted away where it entered the ground and might have fallen if I had leaned on it. "I fix," he said. "I fix tomorrow."

15

We went into the vegetable garden and I pointed to a plot of dirt. "This is my bed," I told Tikhon. I would have liked to tell him that Papa had given this bed to me last spring and that I had raised my own radishes and carrots even though I didn't like to eat carrots. I only liked the way they looked. I also grew flowers for cutting and decorating the house. I would have liked to tell Tikhon all this and more, but it seemed too difficult.

"Mmm," Tikhon said, "you zinnias? Yes?"

How could he know there had been zinnias? They were long out of bloom. He saw my astonishment and picked up a shriveled brown leaf.

"Dis zinnia leaf," he said, "and ere . . . marigold." Then he stroked the stalk of a dried-out sunflower. "Love sunflower. Russia much, much sunflower," he murmured. The sunflower memory seemed to wash the smile off Tikhon's face. For a moment he closed his eyes and stood there looking quite forlorn. I took his hand and pulled him away. Slowly his smile returned.

Before we left the vegetable garden Tikhon picked up a bit of soil and put it in his mouth.

"Tikhon," I cried, "Tikhon!"

He slowly rolled the dirt in his mouth before he spit it out. "Too sour," he announced. "Must fix."

Dirt is not for eating, I thought. I was puzzled, very puzzled, but I didn't say anything. Only later did Papa tell me that "tasting" the soil was an age-old peasant method of finding out what kind of fertilizer the ground needed.

After leaving the vegetable garden, we walked to the end of our property to my favorite tree: a larch. Because of its soft needles and its branches, growing out of the trunk at even intervals, a larch tree is easy to climb. I loved to be high up and look down on our garden, the gardens of our neighbors and the meadows bordering our property. Sometimes I took a book with me. Up there I felt free to recite my favorite poems at the top of my voice, asking the sky and the winds to listen. The tree, however, had one fault. I could climb three quarters of the way to its top, but no farther. Two branches were missing, so the next one was too far up for me to reach. I wanted to show Tikhon what a good climber I was, and in no time I was up. I pointed to where the branches were broken off so Tikhon could see why I couldn't go higher, and then I returned to the ground. Tikhon applauded.

"I too," he said, and quickly he went up. But he stopped before reaching halfway and then, instead of climbing farther he stood up on a branch and let out an earshattering yodel, took his hands off the tree trunk and flung them in the air, and . . . fell down. Only he did not *fall* down; he jumped, landing on his feet, and immediately did three somersaults, landing close to me. He picked me up and whirled me high above his head, then, very gently, put me down on the ground. With his hands on my shoulders, he lowered his head to mine so we were eye to eye and asked, "You like acrobat?"

All this happened in the span of seconds, and I was bewildered, baffled and delighted. What next? I wondered. I caught my breath and eagerly said, "Yes, I do. I do like acrobats."

Chapter Three

That first night of Tikhon's stay in our house, I fell asleep to the faint, quivering sound of his harmonica. The following morning, after a much-too-long Sunday breakfast, my parents got ready for our customary Sunday morning walk.

"I would like to stay home today," I declared, but Papa would not hear of it. "Oh, please," I said. "I would like to be with Tikhon."

19

"Tikhon has work to do," Papa told me. "There is a fence post that needs replacing."

Reluctantly and not enjoying anything, I went along on the walk. When Papa asked me whether I would like to stop at a country inn, I said no, although I knew I was giving up a good cup of hot chocolate with a big pointed heap of whipped cream on top.

As soon as we got home, I looked for Tikhon. He had finished the fence post and was starting to repair a faulty hinge on the garden gate.

"Go climb tree," he said after we had shaken hands.

"Why?" I asked. I wanted to stay close and watch Tikhon work.

"Go," he said. He followed me to the larch tree.

Quickly I climbed up, and when I came to the spot where I could not climb any higher, I found two strong wooden sticks fastened securely to the main trunk. Now I could climb to the next branch with ease. The higher I climbed, the more my view expanded. To my left there was a church steeple I had never seen before. But I could never get to

the top of the tree. The branches there were too thin to hold me, and besides, Tikhon had nailed up a sign: STOP. It was wonderful to be so high up. I called a happy *spasibo* down to Tikhon. *Spasibo* is the Russian word for thank you, which Tikhon had taught me and which was easy to pronounce. Tikhon had learned to say *thank you* from me, but it always came out *tank you*.

Back on the ground I took Tikhon's hand. "Come, I'll show you my brook," I said.

"Brook?" he said, shrugging his shoulders.

"Yes, brook," I said. "Water . . . flowing."

He repeated *brook* and *water flowing*. I led him to the far end of our property. Outside the fence surrounding our grounds ran a narrow, swift brook lined by bushes and willow trees. A large meadow spread beyond. We went through a makeshift little gate and stepped over the brook.

"Easy now," I told Tikhon, "but not easy in spring. Brook too wide and water icy."

Tikhon listened hard. "Say again," he said. I had to repeat it three times before he nodded. But, as so often, I was not sure whether he had understood.

22

A few days later, however, I knew: I found a bridge spanning the brook. Tikhon had fastened two thick boards to short heavy logs, which he had set in the ground on either side of the brook. The bridge was not wide, but long enough and high enough to allow the brook to swell during the rainy season.

"Now I'll be able to walk across with dry feet even when the brook gets much wider," I exclaimed. Remembering that Tikhon could not understand what I was saying, I fell around his neck. *"Spasibo!"* I said. *"Spasibo!"*

That afternoon we sat on the bridge and stared at the sparkling water. After a while Tikhon began to sing softly in Russian. There was only one word I could make out, though I didn't know its meaning: Volga. It appeared time and again and had a melancholy effect on me. "Volga, Volga," I repeated in a low voice after Tikhon had fallen silent again. He squeezed my hand, and as I looked at his face, I saw his eyes were moist.

"Yes, Volga," he said.

Chapter Four

In the days that followed I spent many long hours with Tikhon. We didn't talk much, but it was fun to be with him. He sang while he turned the soil in the vegetable garden; he sang while he dug a ditch; he sang all the time and made work look like play. One day he built a small wheelbarrow for me so I could help him. I learned to say "good morning" and "good night" in Russian, and he learned more German words from me. We exchanged our newly learned words, saying "Good morning" and "Good night" to each other frequently even when it was not morning or evening. And we also liked to look at the Zobten Mountain together. During the summer the Zobten was often shrouded in haze or clouds, but now, in the crisp autumn air, it was visible most of the time.

We had both fallen under the spell of the mountain. We would stand side by side just staring at the triangular shape, whose colors constantly changed.

"It's the weather and the atmosphere," Papa said when I asked him.

But that did not explain my fascination with the beauty of the mountain. I started a little notebook, and every day, half an hour before sunset, I would write down the color of the Zobten and would also try to match it with my colored pencils.

One day I proudly showed my notebook to Mother, but she wasn't very interested and only glanced at the pages. I was so disappointed, I left.

However I continued making my daily entries; I just didn't show them to anybody except Tikhon.

"Watch," I said, pointing to the Zobten.

Tikhon was always eager to look at the Zobten with me.

"Look," I said, "look! Zobten is blue."

I opened my notebook. "But look! Yesterday Zobten was purple."

"Yes, vas," said Tikhon.

Turning back another page, I showed him the color the day before that.

"Aah," Tikhon said, and reached for my notebook. Slowly he turned page after page and took his time to look at each one carefully. When he came to the pink, he got very excited.

"Ink!" he exclaimed. "Ink!"

"Pink," I corrected. "Say pink, Tikhon."

"Pink, I remember. Veek ago. Zobten pink. Very pink."

For a long time he looked at the pink I had put down. He didn't turn to the next page, but bent his head backward and thought. Finally he said, "Pink, yes. But different pink; more yellow in pink."

I handed him the colored pencils I carried in my pocket and said, "Do pink."

27

Tikhon did some more thinking with closed eyes; then he put three strokes of three different colors on top of each other and smeared them with his finger till they fused into one color.

"Vas like dat," he said, authority in his voice. He went on turning the pages of the notebook until he had seen all of them. "Fun," he said, handing it back to me. "Fun. Zobten in pretty coats." And after a moment's silence he added, "I vill do same."

A few days later we had a great time comparing our color notes. Tikhon's were a little more accurate than mine, but he praised mine with an eager nodding of his head or a squeeze of my hand or an emphatic "very very."

One day Tikhon surprised me with a beautiful wooden sled he had built. INGE, surrounded by a garland of flowers, was burned into the wood. Under that was my name in Russian letters. When Tikhon gave me the sled, he pointed to the Zobten and made a long speech, of which I didn't understand a word. But he sounded happy and excited, and his kind blue eyes sparkled.

"Thank you," I said in Russian, *"Spasibo."* I did not know how to say "Very much," but I felt it—much—very much; and I hugged Tikhon.

We sat down on my new sled and looked at the Zobten, blue and beckoning in the distance. After a while Tikhon got up, motioning me to remain seated. He took the rope tied to the front of the sled and began to pull it over the moist, slippery grass. Three times Tikhon pulled me around the blue spruce that stood in the middle of our front lawn.

Every night the comforting sound of Tikhon's harmonica lulled me to sleep, and every night I said good night to the Zobten, sometimes in Russian. In a mysterious way the Zobten did not seem so far away anymore.

Chapter Five

I had always liked the hours of schooling with Mr. Keller, but since the arrival of Tikhon I could hardly wait till the lessons were over and I could join him. One day I wanted to show him Herzel, my favorite doll. Herzel was a baby doll, round and chubby with short curly hair. Once her bright-blue eyes had opened and closed, but I accidentally dropped her and that closed her eyes for good. I vividly remembered the accident and the pain I felt. "Open your eyes! *Please!!*" I begged as I kept shaking her and crying. But her eyelids remained closed. She also lost the thumb on her left hand in that fall, but that I didn't mind as much.

"Dohl, bee-yu-tu-fool dohl," he said when he saw my Herzel.

"Doll, Tikhon," I said. "Say doll."

"Dohl," he said again, as he tenderly held her in his hands. "Herzel" he couldn't say. It came out "Erzel" each time. Suddenly his smile vanished. "Blind?" he asked.

I shook my head. With my little finger I carefully opened one of Herzel's eyelids. When I took my finger away, the lid fell shut.

"Broken?" Tikhon asked.

"Yes," I said, "broken."

"Broken," Tikhon repeated and sadly shook his head. Then, to my surprise, he held Herzel upside down and looked under her skirt.

"I vill try to fix," he said. "Undress!"

I couldn't see why my Herzel had to be undressed so her eyes could be fixed, but reluctantly I did as Tikhon asked. He took her out of my hands and began moving all her joints: her arms, her legs, her head. Then he raised her to his ear and listened.

"Can you hear anything?" I asked.

Tikhon nodded, took a thin wire and inserted it at the shoulder joint. Then he gave it a hard, short pull. *Click-clack* and . . . Herzel's head fell off! I let out a scream.

"No, no," said Tikhon quietly. And so soft, so tender and yet reassuring were these two little words that all my fear left me and was replaced by trust and curiosity.

There lay Herzel's head—bodyless. There was a large hole under the chin where the head had joined the neck, and out of this hole stuck a wire spring.

Tikhon removed the spring and said, "Aaa!"

"Ah what?" I asked.

"Look," he said, and let me peek into the hole. "Look, eyes!"

All I saw were more wires and springs, but Tikhon was beaming. He began to talk excitedly in Russian and, of course, I couldn't understand a word. I sat silently and watched. After a while

Tikhon stopped talking to himself and started to hum, while his big hands moved back and forth.

Everything seemed to take an eternity, and my confidence in Tikhon began to dwindle. There lay the naked, headless body of my Herzel, and Tikhon worked and worked on her head and nothing happened. What if body and head *never* came together again and my Herzel were lost forever?

"Stop!" I cried. "Stop, Tikhon. I want my doll back the way she was. Together!"

"Yes, yes," he murmured, "yes, yes." And he reached for the body and worked another few minutes until body and head were joined. Then he laid her on the table.

I sighed with relief. She looked so sweet with her eyes closed. Why had I ever wanted to change her? I picked her up and pressed her against my heart. Then I stretched out my arms and looked at her. Her eyes were open! Blue and wide, staring back at me.

I gasped.

Tikhon smiled and said, "Yes, yes."

I put Herzel down, and with a light *click* she closed her eyes.

I fell around Tikhon's neck. "Thank you," I said. *"Spasibo!"* I said the words over and over again.

After I dressed Herzel, Tikhon asked, "Finger? You vant Erzel new finger?"

"Can you?" I asked.

Tikhon nodded. "Leave to me for night," he said.

I wanted so much to take Herzel to bed with me that night, but I felt I owed it to her to get her a new thumb as soon as possible.

The next morning when I came down to breakfast, there was Herzel sitting on my chair, open eyed and with all ten fingers.

Chapter Six

November came. The ground froze, and most of the outdoor work was done. But Tikhon had indoor talents, too. He got the huge grandfather clock, which had refused to strike the hour properly for a long time, to strike loud and clear again. He silenced the squeaking of many doors and made the wobbly banister of the staircase sound and safe. But most of his days he spent in his basement room. It seemed to me the melodies on his harmonica got more melancholy as the days grew shorter.

"Don't go into Tikhon's room," Mother told me. "Tikhon needs his privacy."

Of course I respected Tikhon's privacy, but I was still curious to see his room. So one day when Tikhon was in the garden, I peeked through the window.

The room was dark and I couldn't see much. Just beneath the window I could make out a table, with a photograph propped up against a small icon. The photograph showed three horses, held together by a wooden arch, pulling a sleigh. A man and a child wearing high fur hats and covered up to their chests with fur blankets sat in the sleigh. Glittering decorations hung around the horses' necks. Could they be bells? As much as I twisted my neck and strained my eyes, I could not see clearly.

Suddenly Tikhon stood beside me. I was ashamed to be caught peeking. "The horses," I stammered, "the—the three horses under the arch . . . they . . . they are nice."

Tikhon walked away quickly. I was afraid he might be angry with me, but a moment later he was back with the photograph in his hand.

Tikhon pointed to the sleigh. "Dis troika," he said, and, moving his finger to the child, "dis Tikhon." Next he pointed to the man holding the reins in one hand and a long whip in the other. "Papa," he said, and then he pointed to a hill in the background and whispered in my ear: "Zobten!" He looked at me and grinned.

I took time to look carefully at little Tikhon in his fur hat and at Papa Tikhon with the whip. "Bells?" I asked, pointing to the row of shiny globes around the horses' necks. "Bells?"

At first Tikhon did not understand, but when I again pointed to them, he said, "Ding-dong, bimbam." He kept staring and smiling at the photo, and with a sigh he said, "Snow," and added "much" and "bee-yu-tu-fool." He closed his eyes for a moment and repeated, "Bee-yu-tu-fool . . . much . . . vite . . . snow."

There was a great longing in his voice; so I said,

"Soon." I pointed to the snow in the photo and said, "Soon. Snow soon."

And I was right. A few days later the world was white.

I was restless during the morning hours of Mr. Keller's lessons. I couldn't wait to get out to use my new sled. As soon as Mr. Keller left, I got into my winter coat and snow boots, told Mother I was going to try out my new sled and hurried outdoors. Tikhon was already waiting with the sled, as he had promised he would be.

"Ready?" he asked.

I nodded and sat down on the sled. Tikhon took the rope in his hand and began to run. Soundlessly the sled glided through the fluffy snow. Tikhon ran faster. How strong he is, I thought.

After a while Tikhon stopped and turned to me. "Appy?" he asked.

"Happy!" I answered, and we both laughed.

Then Tikhon neighed. "I orse," he said, and when I laughed louder, he neighed louder.

After a while I got up and made Tikhon sit down

on the sled. He didn't want to, but I insisted. Now I brayed, pretending to be a donkey, and for a while I pulled Tikhon. Of course I couldn't run— Tikhon was too heavy—but we moved. I looked back often. Tikhon sat quite erect on the sled. His legs were crossed under his body and his arms were folded across his chest. He was smiling and humming.

A short time later Tikhon made me sit on the sled again, and he trotted on, neighing every so often. In front of us was the Zobten, clearly outlined against the bright-blue sky. It was beautiful! I wished the ride would never end.

Suddenly Tikhon stopped and looked at me. "Zobten?" he asked.

"Yes." I nodded. "Yes, Zobten."

Tikhon started pulling again, but now there was determination in his gait. He had stopped neighing and seldom looked back at me. I could feel a change had come over him, and slowly I realized the Zobten was like a magnet pulling him on. Hadn't he told me there was a mountain resembling the Zobten near his home in Russia? And now, I thought,

40

the snow-swept fields surrounding us must remind him of the long, snowy Russian winters.

I looked around and saw the colors change. The snow took on a bluish hue where the shadows fell. And our own shadows on the snow were long, very long. I turned back and saw the sun close to the horizon.

"Tikhon," I called, "I think we should turn back."

Tikhon had not heard me, so I called again. But he continued his even pace, marching straight ahead.

I got up and pulled on his jacket. "Tikhon, it's getting late," I said. "The sun is going down. We should go home now."

"Ome," he repeated, not taking his eyes off the Zobten, "ome."

"Yes," I pleaded, "let's turn back."

He stopped and I thought he had understood. But he did not turn back. He only looked at me and said, "You—I—Zobten," and went on walking.

What does he mean? I wondered. Does he want us to walk all the way to the Zobten? Right now?

I did not want to sit on the sled anymore. I walked beside Tikhon and talked to him. I put my hand in his; he gave it a squeeze, and again he said, "You—I—Zobten." This time he laughed and his laugh frightened me a little.

"Tikhon," I urged, "I want home! I am hungry!"

Tikhon patted his belly and said, "Ungry too." Then he pulled some money out of his pocket and said, "You—I—eat." He shielded his eyes against the glow of the setting sun and looked all around. "Look," he said, pointing to a church steeple to our right.

"Let's go there," I said. "We will find a telephone in the village, and I can call Mother and tell her not to worry."

But Tikhon did not hear what I said. I said it again, but Tikhon paid no attention. He continued his even pace toward the Zobten. Not knowing what else I could do, I trotted along beside him. A few minutes later another church steeple pierced the sky. In this part of Silesia's countryside, village is close to village, and it never takes more than half an hour to walk from one to the next. This village was directly in front of us in one line with the Zobten, and therefore found Tikhon's approval.

"Good," he declared. "You—I—dere eat." He waved at the Zobten, heaved a mammoth sigh and mumbled, "Zobten must vait."

By now the Zobten Mountain had turned purple. Only the very tip of it had an orange glow, reflecting the last beams of the setting sun.

Chapter Seven

We reached the village and found an inn. As we
entered a smoke-filled, noisy room and sat down
at a table, the noise stopped and everybody stared
at us. I would have liked to disappear down a
mousehole, but Tikhon did not seem to mind.
Nudging my elbow, he said, "Get bread—get sausage—get cheese. And get beer." After I had ordered, Tikhon smiled and patted my hand. Soon
the innkeeper put a tall glass of beer on the table.

Tikhon took a long swallow, licked his lips and pushed the glass in front of me. "Try," he said, "try. Is good."

I took a sip. It tasted awful! But Tikhon liked it; he laughed—it made him happy. He drank one glass after another, and the more he drank the more he laughed.

Then he pulled his harmonica out of his vest and started to play. The other guests fell silent; they listened and applauded. That gave Tikhon courage, and he played more and louder. The innkeeper put another tall glass of beer in front of Tikhon and refused to accept money for it. Tikhon gulped the beer down in one long swallow and everyone applauded. When the innkeeper brought our bread and cheese, Tikhon was not in the mood to eat anymore. Instead, he got up and—still playing the harmonica—started to dance.

It was a wild dance. He jumped in the air—he kicked his heels—he stamped his feet. He squatted close to the floor while kicking his legs in all directions. It frightened me a bit, but everybody else enjoyed it tremendously. Several people even stood up to see Tikhon better, and the innkeeper pushed some empty tables to the wall to make more room for Tikhon.

But Tikhon did not need more room. To prove it, he jumped on top of a table and continued his dance there. The onlookers were delighted. They clapped their hands and started stamping their feet. Tikhon's face turned red, and beads of sweat formed on his forehead.

"Come!" I called, and pointed to the food on our table, but Tikhon kept dancing. "Come back and eat," I begged. But Tikhon grabbed me and pulled me up on the table with him. He lifted me in the air and whirled me around until I was dizzy. By now the applause was tremendous.

"Give him more beer on me!" someone shouted.

"On me too!" called another voice.

"Help!" I screamed.

The innkeeper came forward and freed me from Tikhon's grip.

"You'd better eat now," he said, and sat down beside me, but he didn't take his eyes off the dancing Tikhon.

I couldn't eat; I was too dizzy.

The innkeeper turned to me. "Who is he?" he asked.

I didn't know what to answer, so I pretended to have a little coughing fit. But when I was through coughing, the innkeeper asked again, "Who is he?"

To my surprise I heard myself say, "My uncle." Inside myself I said, *Forgive me, God, for lying.*

"He does not speak our language," the innkeeper said.

"No, he doesn't," I replied.

"Why?" the innkeeper wanted to know.

I had no answer to that, so I folded my arms on the table and put my head down. "I'm so dizzy," I murmured. "I'm so tired."

The innkeeper got up and left the room. A moment later he came back with a woman at his side. "My wife will take you upstairs," he said.

A firm, warm hand took mine, and for a moment I felt I was safe. We went upstairs, where the innkeeper's wife put me on a sofa and tucked me under a heavy blanket.

"There," she said, "there. Now sleep, child." She

went to the door and shut off the light, but before she left, she asked, "What is your name, child?"

"Inge," I answered.

"Inge what?" she asked.

Fear filled my brain. Wouldn't it be better—for Tikhon's sake—if I didn't give my real name? So I said, "Inge Stein." But in a lower voice, so low that nobody but God could hear me, I said, *Forgive me for lying again.*

"And where do you come from?"

"Please," I said and made my voice tremble, "please let me sleep now. I'm *so* tired."

"All right, child," the woman said tenderly. "All right. You will tell me tomorrow."

She shut the door and I was alone. Alone in a strange room in a strange house in a strange village, surrounded by strangers. I was not tired at all. I was too excited and too worried to be sleepy. I also wanted to talk to Mother, but I had not seen a telephone. And I was hungry. My stomach growled. I should have taken some bread and cheese with me, but now it was too late. I couldn't go back downstairs. They would ask me more ques-

tions. All I could do now was lie here and wait.
Wait for what? Well—wait till . . . till I got an idea.
I had to think of *something* to get Tikhon and me
out of this place.

The room I was in must have been directly over
the public room of the inn, because I could hear
the clapping of hands, the stamping of feet and,
every once in a while, Tikhon's laughter. How will
it all end? I asked myself. I was worried about
Mother and worried about her worrying about me.

I was still thinking hard when the door opened
and the innkeeper and his wife entered quietly.
With candles in their hands they stepped close to
the sofa. I kept my eyes shut.

"Yes," the woman whispered, "she is asleep now."

"Poor child," her husband whispered.

"Have you called the police?" asked the woman.

"Not yet. I'll do it in the morning," the innkeeper answered.

The police, I thought. The *POLICE!* And I started
to tremble.

50

Chapter Eight

I must have fallen asleep, because the next thing I knew there was complete silence and darkness. Now, I thought, the whole house must be asleep. And indeed I heard someone snore in the room next door. A pale rectangle on one wall told me where the window was. I got up and felt my way toward it. It wasn't pitch dark outdoors, and I could vaguely make out other buildings surrounding the inn and a few tall fir trees. I could also see the church steeple, but I couldn't read its clock. I wondered how late it was and where Tikhon was.

Suddenly the church bell rang. Four strokes. Had I ever been up at four o'clock in the morning? I couldn't remember. The last of the four strokes still vibrated in the air when a dog answered it; a long howl, eerily filling the night.

Where is Tikhon? Where is Tikhon? The question hammered in my mind. Besides, I was dreadfully hungry. My last meal had been yesterday's breakfast. Maybe the bread and cheese were still downstairs, I thought, and I decided to find my way to them. I searched for the door and found it. I moved inch by inch until I reached the stairs, and step by step I tiptoed down. A dim shaft of light helped me make out a door. I opened it, and by the awful smell of smoke and beer I knew I was entering the right room.

It was completely dark. I knew it was a large room and I remembered it had several doors. At which door was I now? And where was the table at which Tikhon and I had sat and where I hoped to find the bread and cheese I had not eaten? The table was in a corner, I remembered, and there was a wooden bench running along three of the four walls of the room. I felt for the bench, and slowly and cautiously let the bench guide me. For a few minutes—every move took a long time—I slid along the bench. Suddenly I flinched. My hand, testing ahead of me, touched something. Something soft. A pillow, I thought, and I remembered there were some pillows scattered along the hard wooden benches.

I put my hand flat on the pillow—and the pillow jerked! I let out a cry. My cry was answered by a low growl, followed by a grunt, a sound I knew. My fingers felt what my eyes could not see: rough, short, curly hair; broad shoulders; fur-lined vest.

"Tikhon," I whispered, "Tikhon."

The answer was a grunt. I shook Tikhon. First gently, then roughly. But Tikhon slept on. His head felt hot and he smelled like a barrel of beer. I shook him again and pinched him. Tikhon slept on. All I could do was sit and wait.

He will wake up eventually, I comforted myself. And now I felt the hunger again. I remembered

Tikhon always carried matches in his pocket. I reached into his pocket, found a match and lit it.

There was nothing on the table but a tall empty bottle. V O D K A, the label said. I lit another match and walked toward the counter from which the innkeeper had served the drinks and food earlier in the evening. Maybe there is something to eat, I hoped. And indeed there was: In a large glass jar were hard-boiled, pickled eggs.

I took one out and ate it. I ate another one and another. I couldn't stop. I ate five all together.

Then I walked back to Tikhon, lit another match and looked at him. He lay on his side, curled up on the hard wooden bench, his knees nearly touching his chin. He puffed and snored and sometimes moaned. I sat down beside him.

Time passed, how long I didn't know. I didn't pay attention to the strokes of the church clock. But when I saw the windows filled with pale, pale blue, I knew we had to leave before morning and before the police arrived. With all my might I shook Tikhon, and when he didn't wake up, I twisted his nose and pulled his ears.

Suddenly he popped up like a jack-in-the-box. He rubbed his eyes. He stretched his back. He groaned.

I put my hand over his mouth. "Hush," I said, "hush."

He blinked his eyes, looked around and tried to shake himself awake. Again he wanted to say something, but I wouldn't let him. I pushed and pulled and made him stand up.

"Come," I said, "we *must* leave before the police arrive."

Tikhon stared at me with a stupefied smile. Did he understand? No, he did not. He fell back onto the bench, mumbling something I couldn't understand. I was desperate. Then I had an idea. "Come, Tikhon," I said softly, "come. Zobten waits."

A change came over Tikhon. He cleared his throat. "Yes," he said, ". . . you—I—Zobten." We got our coats from the clothes tree, and I wanted to leave, but Tikhon held me back.

"Vait," he said. He took money out of his pocket and put a few bills on the table. When we passed the serving counter, he put another bill down and took a few pickled eggs out of the glass jar. He wrapped them carefully in his red handkerchief and shoved them into his pocket. "Honest," he said, "me honest."

I led him to the door. He was not very steady on his feet.

As we stepped outside, the cold air hit us. Tikhon staggered forward and nearly fell. It was easy for me to press him down onto the sled, but not so easy for me to pull the sled and walk fast. I had only one thought: to get out of the village as quickly as possible before daybreak, and before the police arrived.

The fresh air did Tikhon good. He seemed to come to his senses. He even began to hum, and a short time later he got off the sled and took the rope out of my hand.

"Now I," he said. "Tank you, mademoiselle."

But I didn't want to sit on the sled. All I wanted was to put as much distance as possible between the inn and us. After we had walked for some time, I began to relax. I let myself look around me, and realized that we were headed for the Zobten again.

Now, in the sober light of morning my conscience began to stir again. I thought of Mother worrying and hoped that Tikhon's desire to climb the Zobten had left him.

I pointed to the Zobten. "No, Tikhon, *not* Zobten!" I cried. "Home!"

I started to walk away from Tikhon and the Zobten, but Tikhon did not follow me.

"Come," I called over my shoulder.

No answer.

I looked back. Tikhon just stood there looking at the mountain. I walked back to face him. I was not prepared for what I saw: tears ran down his cheeks.

"Tikhon," I said tenderly, "Tikhon."

"Zobten," he whispered, "Zobten so close. Zobten so bee-yu-tu-fool. Like ome." And after a moment's silence, he added, "Zobten . . . my eart." He pressed one hand on his chest and reached for mine with the other. "You—I—bee-yu-tu-fool Zobten," he said over and over. And each time he said it, the Zobten became more desirable for me, too.

The sun came up behind the mountain like a

halo around its peak and made the sky sparkle. It melted away all resistance within me.

"You—I—climb," Tikhon whispered as he stamped his feet and bent forward and breathed heavily as if climbing. "Den, top. Aaah!" Slowly he spun around and, with a grand gesture, pointed out the view. "Aaah," he said again, his face glowing. He pulled out some coins from his pocket and showed them to me in his flat hand. "Den mountain restaurant! Lemonade! Cake! Vodka!"

"No vodka," I said, but Tikhon didn't hear me. He threw his arms into the air and jumped up and down like a child.

"And den—DE BEST! Den sled down! *Whiff! Whoosh!*" He whistled like the wind, ruffling his hair with his hands. "You—I—fly on sled—down!" Tikhon's face was sunnier than the rising sun!

He was so happy! And I was happy too.

The climb up the mountain was strenuous but beautiful. Frequently Tikhon would stop to point out a sharp curve in the road. "Slow," he would say, "very slow." When the road came close to a steep ravine, Tikhon stopped, looked around and repeated, "Slow." I understood. He wanted to mark these spots in his memory so they would give him a warning on the downhill ride. I knew I could trust Tikhon, and yet a mixture of fear and delight prickled within me.

We reached the top around noon. We walked around the mountain inn and looked in all directions and smiled at each other. It was beautiful!

Below us flat land, dotted with many villages, spread to the west. A river, looking like a black snake in the snow, meandered from village to village. To the east a gentle chain of hills gradually flattened and, far in the distance, melted together with the wide sky.

As we stood and watched, Tikhon broke into something he called the "Volga Song."

"It sounds sad," I said.

Tikhon nodded, but said, "I no sad now. I glad!" He laughed.

I was happy too, and I knew the *best* was still to come.

But first we wanted a rest. It was cozy and warm inside the mountain inn. A fire crackled in an open fireplace, and the burning pinecones smelled delicious. We found an empty table in a corner by a window and ordered hot chocolate for me and tea for Tikhon. We also ordered bread and butter, and Tikhon insisted on some ham. He unwrapped the pickled eggs and we had a feast. We both were very hungry. Between bites we looked out the window.

Some clouds had formed in the bright-blue sky and they came sailing straight toward us. They came so fast that within minutes they reached the top of the mountain, and suddenly we were engulfed in a shimmering, foaming, milky fog and had lost the world beneath us. Bewildered, I looked at Tikhon.

"Dis not end of vorld," he said. "Vill pass."

And as fast as the clouds had covered all and everything around the inn, just as fast they passed and gave us back the clear, wide view of the world below us.

We finished eating, but neither of us wanted to

leave. I, for one, felt like stretching the joy of anticipating the downhill ride. So we ordered more tea and chocolate and some cake, too.

"All this on *top* of the Zobten," I said.

Tikhon did not understand, but cheerfully repeated, "Yes, Zobten."

The Zobten in its winter coat had been nothing but a faraway blue hump on the horizon to me, not even visible every day; but now it belonged to me, and somehow I felt I belonged to it.

"How long will the downhill ride take?" I asked Tikhon, but he didn't understand. I had to repeat and rephrase.

When Tikhon finally understood, he shrugged his shoulders. He squinted his eyes as he always did when he thought hard. Then he flashed his ten fingers at me twice and said, "Mi-noo-tes."

"Twenty minutes?" I asked.

He tilted his head from one shoulder to the other to suggest he wasn't quite sure. Then he flashed one hand three times.

"Fifteen minutes only?" I asked.

A nod and a shrug were Tikhon's answer.

Chapter Nine

I could hardly wait for the moment when we would sit on the sled and start the ride down. Finally Tikhon got up and said, "Now!"

My heart beat faster. I was so excited my arms couldn't find the armholes in my coat and Tikhon had to help me. We walked toward the door, but the door opened before we reached it and two men came in. We wanted to pass them and leave, but they stepped in our way.

"Stop," the taller one said.

The other one reached into his pocket and pulled out a silver badge. He held it up to Tikhon and said, "Police."

I grabbed Tikhon's hand; it trembled. The man with the badge said something that neither Tikhon nor I understood.

When the innkeeper came up to us, the tall policeman said, "Sorry, we have to arrest these two."

"Why?" asked the innkeeper.

"Because," said the policeman, "they fit the description we got from the girl's mother and from the innkeeper at the village where they spent last night. Have they paid their bill?"

"*Of course* we have!" I answered, getting very angry. And seeing handcuffs in the policeman's hand, I declared, "You don't need them. We will go with you."

They led us to a van and we climbed in.

"The sled!" I cried, suddenly remembering.

"We don't need a sled," the tall policeman said.

"It's my sled," I cried. "Tikhon made it for me.

We can't leave it behind." And I jumped out of the van.

The policeman jumped after me. What did he think? I was going to run away? I would *never* leave Tikhon behind.

"Go back," said the policeman. "I'll get your sled. Which one is it?"

"The one with the roses around my name," I said proudly. "My name is Inge."

"I know," the policeman grumbled, as he went and picked up the sled.

The tall policeman got into the driver's seat, and the other one joined Tikhon and me in the back. He sat down on the narrow bench along the side wall of the van and motioned us to sit beside him. Tikhon was quite ready to obey, but I took Tikhon's hand and pulled him down to sit with me on our sled. The engine started to rattle and the van began to move. Slowly it wound its way downhill. Tikhon and I sat hand in hand. We did not speak. At least not words. But when we looked into each other's eyes, we knew each other's thoughts. We were going downhill sitting on our sled. But *how* different it

was from the way we had imagined it would be! We didn't even try to look out. The two small windows were too high up anyway.

How long we rode I couldn't tell. When the van stopped in front of our house, only I was let out. Mother came running and pulled me into her arms.

She sobbed, "Are you all right, child?"

"Of course I am all right," I answered.

The policeman brought my sled and talked at length with Mother. Then he asked her to sign a paper. I wanted to wait for Tikhon, but Mother pulled me into the house. "Stay here," she said, and hurried off.

I looked out the window. The van's door was closed, and the tall policeman was putting a heavy iron lock on it.

Then he climbed into the driver's seat and started the engine. For a second I saw Tikhon's face behind the iron bars of the small window.

As the van was pulling away, Mother came running to the door, calling, "Hold it! Wait!" But nobody but me could hear her. Mother stood there looking helpless and sad. In her trembling hands she clutched Manya, Tikhon's beautiful turtle. She handed the turtle to me. "It's yours now," she said. "I guess it's yours now."

Chapter Ten

I sat down with the turtle in my lap. Mother came and sat down beside me. I could tell from her face she had not slept and had probably wept all night. Slowly, step by step, I told her everything.

"Forgive me," I begged after I had finished. "I should have phoned. But everything was so exciting and everything happened so fast."

Mother nodded.

"What will happen to Tikhon now?" I asked.

"Right now I do not care," Mother said. "All I care about is having you back unharmed."

I let go of the turtle and put my arms around Mother's neck. "But Mama," I stammered, "why did you call the police? You know that Tikhon . . ."

"I had to, my darling," she said. "I had to! Don't you understand? I was out of my mind with worry. When it got pitch dark and you weren't back yet . . ."

"But Mama, I was with Tikhon. You knew I was safe."

"I tried to tell myself that. But as it got later and later I became frantic. I had to do something. I couldn't go out and look for you. I didn't know where to start. So I called the police. You must understand that, Inge."

I tried to, but I couldn't. Why do grownups always worry so much? Why can't they believe things will turn out all right like I do? That night I lay awake for a long time thinking about Tikhon and wondering what would happen to him.

We did not go to Tikhon's room until Papa came home on Saturday. After Mother and I told him

what had happened, the three of us went downstairs.

We opened the door to Tikhon's room and just
stood there on the threshold. The room was
clean and orderly. Beside his simple bed there
was a small night table that Tikhon had made
himself. A three-forked branch that Tikhon had
changed into a candlestick and a tin mug filled
with dried autumn flowers stood on the table.
On the wall hung a small bookshelf with beautifully carved endpieces. There were two books
on it; a small Russian Bible and a very worn,
cardboard-bound beginners' German grammar
and dictionary.

Little paper strips stuck out of the dictionary at
various spots. Papa opened it at a marked page,
smiled and handed the dictionary to me. Many
words were underlined in red: *thank—thankful—
thought—timid—tree*. I turned the pages to another marker. More red underlinings: *lonely—
longing—love*. And: *father—far—fear—forever*. I
closed the book.

I looked at the table under the window. The

small icon was still there, the photo leaning against it.

"This is Tikhon with his father," I explained.

One corner of the room was shielded by a large three-panel screen. Behind the screen we found neatly arranged carpenter's tools and a big table improvised with boards over two wooden horses. And then I gasped! One the table stood a dollhouse. A big dollhouse. But not *just* a dollhouse. It was *our* house! All the rooms were furnished with miniatures of our furniture. We stared in astonishment.

"Look how pretty the dining room is," Mother exclaimed.

"And my writing desk in the study," said Papa.

We walked around to the back of the little house, and there were the kitchen downstairs and the bedrooms upstairs.

"But look!" I exclaimed. "Look at my room."

"It is empty," said Papa.

"Yes, empty," I said in disappointment.

———

We all missed Tikhon, but I missed him the most.

"Where is Tikhon now?" I kept asking Papa, but Papa would not say. I was not sure whether he didn't know or whether he didn't want to tell me. But I kept asking until finally Papa said, "Tikhon has been living in Germany without papers, as you know. The police found out when they caught up with you on the Zobten, and they are holding him. He did not commit a crime, but . . ." Papa hesitated. "It is against regulations. You understand?"

"No," I said, "I don't understand."

Papa put his hands on my shoulders and said, "Inge, I want you not to worry about Tikhon so much. I'm doing everything I can to help him, and I hope in six months you will see him again. That's all I can tell you now."

I stopped asking, but every day I went down to Tikhon's room and looked at the dollhouse and wondered why my room was the only one that was empty. I also looked at Tikhon's photo through a magnifying glass and saw how beautifully the horse-drawn sleigh was decorated. But I did not disturb anything.

When he comes back, I thought, he should find everything the way he left it.

Chapter Eleven

As days passed I missed Tikhon more and more, and I spent hours in his room with Manya, the turtle. One day Papa told me, "You'd better find a soft spot in the garden and let Manya dig a hole for her winter sleep. That's what turtles do when winter comes."

But I wouldn't have any part of it. Manya was a living link to Tikhon. I had even renamed her secretly, and when nobody was within earshot, I called her Tikhon. Papa brought me a book about turtles and after I had read it carefully, I knew I had to let her hibernate. I waited for a mild day and took her to the vegetable garden; I set Manya-Tikhon on the ground.

"Sleep tight," I said. "See you next spring." And without turning back I went into the house.

I spent hours staring at the dollhouse. The emptiness of my room continued to puzzle me. "Why, Tikhon, why?" I kept asking. One day I was so desperate I shook the whole house. All the furniture slid out of place, and it took me a long time to put it back where it belonged. Then I threw myself on Tikhon's bed.

A little while later I got up. I lifted the pillow to fluff it up and found a flat book underneath. It was a sketchbook, tied shut by two strings. I knew I should not pry into other people's property, but I couldn't resist opening it.

Tikhon's name was printed on the first page in ornate letters. Drawings of flowers and trees with their Russian and German names followed. Then came a page with pressed, dried flowers. Though their colors had faded, their delicate beauty was preserved. The following pages were filled with sketches of our furniture. Page after page. How well he can draw, I thought. Then I came to a page filled with words only. Words he must have copied out of the dictionary. To the left the Russian words, unreadable for me (Why did they have to have such different letters?), and to the right the German words. INGE was written at the top of the page in the same fancy lettering as on my sled. It was followed by *heaven—home—heart—house—harvest—homesick—haven—hope*. I was not sure why the words moved me so, but they did; and I read them over several times.

Then I turned the page and saw a big drawing filling a double page. It was the inside of a room. A room so pretty I gasped. There was a four-poster bed with ruffled curtains. The posts were heavily carved; leaves and blossoms wound around them. A fur rug with a pair of embroidered slippers on it lay beside the bed. Wooden logs burned in an open fireplace with an even larger fur rug in front of it. Glassed-in bookshelves lined the walls, and a parrot sat in an ornate wire cage. Vases filled with flowers were everywhere. Then I saw a vanity table. It was larger and much prettier than Mother's, with ruffles all around it. A young woman sat in front of it. Her long blond hair flowed down her back and nearly touched the floor. I looked at her face reflected in the mirror. Didn't it look a little like mine? No. I had to laugh at myself—I wasn't that pretty. Many little things covered the vanity table. A big powder puff, much larger than Mother's. A round box on three graceful feet with sculpted flowers for a lid. A hand mirror with an extra-long handle, also beautifully decorated and with the initials I.S. on the back. My initials! As I looked closer still, I found many more I.S.'s everywhere. They were woven into all the decorations. I was dumbfounded! I had seen rooms like this only in fairy-tale books, inhabited by princesses and queens. Was this what Tikhon wished for me?

"Oh, Tikhon," I cried, "oh, Tikhon, Tikhon." I buried my face in my hands, and for the first time since the police had taken Tikhon away, I wept.

Chapter Twelve

"Can I have a lesson about Russia?" I asked Mr. Keller the next morning.

"All right," he said. "I will work it into your geography lesson next week."

"No, no," I said, "today."

Mr. Keller did not like this idea. He had arrived late and his eyes seemed redder than usual. His nose too.

"But Inge," he said, "it is a big country and it is a big subject. I must prepare myself for it."

"*Please*," I insisted, "Just tell me something you know about Russia. Anything. Right now!"

Mr. Keller took off his glasses and polished them for an eternity. "Well . . ." he began, then stopped and polished his glasses again. "Well . . . there is the Volga. But that, of course, you know."

"No, I don't know the Volga," I said, but then I remembered I had heard the word in Tikhon's songs. "What is the Volga?" I asked.

"Aaah," said Mr. Keller, "the Volga! The Volga is a river. A *big* river; wide and long. Much longer than any river we have in Germany. And the Russians *love* their Volga. It is as dear to their hearts as their blood to their veins. It carries ships and boats and rafts. They have hundreds of stories and many, many songs about it. And when they are away from Russia, they seem to long for the Volga just as you would long for your father and mother if they were far away." Then he asked me to get the atlas and he showed me the Volga. "Tomorrow

I will bring you pictures of the Volga and the towns and villages along its banks, but now we have to have the planned lesson in arithmetic." He closed the atlas and talked arithmetic.

But I stayed with the Volga; Tikhon's Volga. And whatever Mr. Keller said went in one ear and out the other without leaving a trace in my brain.

For days and days thoughts of Tikhon filled my head. Where was he? What was he doing and what was he thinking? Papa and Mother avoided talking about him. Every day I went down to Tikhon's basement room, opened his drawing pad and looked at the room of my future. That's what it had become to me: my future room. I did not show it to Mother or Papa. It was a secret. Something I shared only with Tikhon.

Chapter Thirteen

Four weeks had passed since Tikhon's departure. Mr. Keller had shown me pictures of Russian villages, Russian towns and Russian people. He had told me about the old Russia and the splendor of the czars who had ruled Russia. Then one day he said, "That is enough of Russia; other subjects are more important for you to learn now." He pulled a curtain over Russia, but my steadily growing desire to know as much as possible about Russia was not quenched.

The Volga flowed into my dreams together with the melodies of Tikhon's harmonica. One night the melodies were louder and clearer than ever. I awoke as dawn was breaking and sat up in bed. The music continued. I shook my head and rubbed my eyes to clear away the dream; but the music didn't end. It seemed to come from outside my window. I went to the window and looked down.

It was too dark to see anything, but there was no mistaking the harmonica music.

"Tikhon," I called in a hushed voice. "Tikhon, I will be downstairs in a minute."

I slipped into my coat and rushed downstairs, right into Tikhon's open arms. He lifted me from the ground and whirled me around and around. Then he noticed my bedroom slippers.

"Too cold for feets," he said. "Can ve go my room?"

I nodded eagerly. Tikhon sat me down on the bed, tucked a blanket around my feet and pulled up a chair for himself beside me. I was so full of questions, I didn't know where to begin.

"I'm so happy you are back," I said, "but how did you get here?"

"On my feets," he answered.

"Where do you come from?"

"Town," he said. He lowered his eyes and added, "Prison."

"Wonderful," I said. "They let you go!"

"No," he muttered in a voice so low I could hardly hear him.

Suddenly I didn't want to ask any more questions, but Tikhon looked at me and said, "I outbroke."

"How?" I wanted to know. "Won't they be after you?"

He nodded. "Yes." And then he started to talk, fast and confused. It was hard for me to follow. All I understood were repetitions of "Vill die in prison—lonesome. So longing for ome—longing Volga. In prison people mean, people cruel. Omesick—eart vill break."

85

I *never* had heard Tikhon talk so long without interruption. He looked so tired. His knuckles turned white, his face got red.

"Tikhon," I said, "why don't you lie down now?"

"Can *not* lie down in bed—must ask Papa first," he said.

"He is still asleep," I said.

"Vill vait," Tikhon replied.

He told me that he had walked nights and had hidden in barns, stables and basements during the days. It had taken him four nights to get here and he had had nothing to eat; just a handful of raw oats he had found in a horse stable. "I not steal from people," he assured me.

"What now?" I asked.

"Talk to Papa," Tikhon answered. Suddenly he jumped up, lifted me and took me to the window. "Look!" he exclaimed. "Look!" There was the Zobten, surrounded by the first glow of the rising sun. We stared at it till the sun cleared the mountain and blinded our eyes.

"*Bee-yu-tu-fool* Zobten," Tikhon murmured. I heard the tears in his voice and didn't dare look at him. The dark basement room was aglow; the icon on the table sparkled. Tikhon knelt down before it and said a Russian prayer.

I left. I wanted to be in my room in case Papa woke up early and opened the door. I had to wait a long time. Finally the door was opened. I slipped in and quietly sat down beside him.

"Where is the hug and the kiss and the giggle?" he asked, opening just one eye.

"Look at me, Papa," I said. "I want to ask you something."

"Go ahead, darling," he said, "but not before I get my Saturday-morning kiss."

I kissed him quickly. "Papa . . . could Tikhon stay with us *if* he came back?" I blurted out.

Papa shook his head. "It's impossible for him to come back. Tikhon is in prison. We did not want to tell you, knowing it would upset you."

"Maybe they let him go free," I said, my voice very unsure.

"Not before six months are over," Papa said.

"Maybe he'll break out of prison."

"That would be terrible," Papa said. "It would

87

make matters worse for him."

I ignored this last remark and said, "He can break out and run away from the cruel people in prison. He can walk nights and hide in the daytime till he is here. He can sleep in barns and stables and feed himself on a handful of raw oats—because he would not steal from people . . ."

"Well, well," said Papa, "you have worked this out pretty well for Tikhon, haven't you?" And he pulled me close to kiss me.

I freed myself from his arms. "No," I said, "I have not."

Papa looked puzzled, but he smiled. "I wish you wouldn't think so much about this. I also feel very sorry for Tikhon. I have written petitions to the prison warden and even to the governor, but I got only negative answers. Tikhon will have to stay in prison for six months. We can help him to get home after he is released."

"No," I said again, "we must help him now!"

"How?" asked Papa. "They won't even let me talk to him."

Slowly, emphasizing every word, I said, "You

can talk to him. Tikhon is downstairs—in his basement room."

Papa sat up abruptly and looked at me. "You aren't making this up, Inge?" he asked.

"No—he *is* here!"

Hastily Papa got dressed and went downstairs. I wanted to go with him, but he ordered me to stay in my room until he called me. Mother came out of the kitchen, "What's wrong?" she called.

"Tikhon," Papa answered, and without turning his head, closed the basement door with a bang behind him.

Mother saw my frightened face and came upstairs. I told her everything.

"That's bad," she said over and over. "That's really bad . . . for all of us."

I began to feel terrible, too. Mother stayed with me, stroking my hair. We sat in silence. Only when the smell of burned rolls penetrated the room did Mother dash back to the kitchen.

I got dressed and waited. It seemed an eternity till Papa called me down. Mother prepared a tray loaded with rolls, sausage and cheese and a big pot of tea. "Take this to Tikhon," she said, handing me the tray.

I found Tikhon sitting on his bed, elbows on his knees, his face covered with his big hands.

"Mama sent you breakfast, Tikhon," I said.

He nodded without looking at me. "Tank you, little angel. Tank you. And tank Mama."

I put the tray on the table and left.

Half an hour later Papa, Mother and I sat down to our breakfast. We ate in silence. When we finished, Mother asked Papa, "What decision have you come to?"

Papa mumbled, paused and said, "Of course, we can't keep Tikhon here. I told him I would have to drive him back at once. He must return to prison voluntarily. I told him so, very sternly, but . . ." Papa's voice fell into a mumble again, saying something neither Mother nor I could understand.

"Speak more clearly," Mother pleaded, and Papa went on ". . . but when Tikhon started to weep, like a little baby . . . Tikhon, this big, strong man . . . when he fell down on his knees and threw

his arms around my legs *begging* me to let him
stay at least a few days . . . I broke down and promised . . . a few days." Papa stopped talking and
looked from Mother's face to mine and back to
Mother's. We both had tears in our eyes but tried
to smile. Papa reached over the table and put one
hand on one of Mother's and the other one on mine.

"I know, it is not right what I am doing," he
said earnestly. "It might be right in front of God—
but it is *not* right in front of the law." And turning
to Mother, he added, "I know he has given you a
terrible scare, my dear, the night of their foolhardy
escapade. You were furious at Tikhon, but you for-
gave him knowing that Tikhon did not *mean* to
harm Inge or you or anybody."

"Yes," Mother interrupted, "I know Tikhon is a
good person. Only . . . he himself is just a big child."

"Indeed he is," Papa agreed, "and now the poor
fellow is being punished for being an alien without
papers. So we must be careful. Tikhon cannot leave
the basement during the day. He must not be seen
by anybody. He can step out for some fresh air
after dark. We will feed him well and let him catch

up on his sleep. Then, at the latest next Friday, I will drive him back to prison."

Mother and I sighed with relief. Papa's voice took on its normal pitch as he suggested we go for a walk.

Chapter Fourteen

When we returned from our walk, Mother and I took lunch down to Tikhon.

Mother put down the tray and stretched out her hand to Tikhon. He bent down to kiss Mother's hand again and again, stammering words that sounded like "Thanks" and "Forgiveness" and "Bless you" and "Thanks" and more "Thanks." Mother smiled, but was in a hurry to leave the room. She grabbed my hand and pulled me with her. Turning back, I saw Tikhon's face sadden.

"Why can't I stay with Tikhon?" I asked.

"Later," Mother said. "Later you can take supper down to him. Right now go upstairs to your room." Mother's tone left no room for argument.

As I walked slowly up the stairs, I could hear Papa's voice. "Tell me, why won't you let Inge be with Tikhon?"

"Oh, dear," Mother replied, "you men don't understand anything. Don't you know how attached the child is to Tikhon? And how heartbroken she will be when he leaves? I simply want to protect her from that."

Entering my room, I looked at my dolls, sitting in a row on their little bench. Never before had their staring eyes seemed so empty to me; even Herzel's open eyes could not give me comfort. I wanted to be with Tikhon. I wanted to ask him about my future room in the dollhouse. I wanted to confess I had seen the sketchbook under his pillow. Ask him to tell me more about Russia and the Volga. I dragged out my atlas and looked at the map of the world. How large Russia was! With a piece of paper, cut vaguely in the shape of Germany, I tried to figure out how many times Germany would fit into Russia. It didn't quite work out right, but I could see it fitted many, many times.

The afternoon seemed without end, but finally I heard Mother calling and I hurried downstairs. She handed me a heavily loaded tray and opened the door to the basement. "Be careful now" was all she said.

I took every step slowly, but before I was half-way down, Tikhon opened his door and, smiling happily, relieved me of the heavy tray. After he had folded his hands for a short silent prayer, he ate. I sat there, watching his joy in eating. I was happy to be with him again.

When I heard Mother's voice calling me I tried to ignore her, but Tikhon said, "Mama—she calls—you go."

I didn't get up. She had *promised* I could be with Tikhon.

"You *must* go," Tikhon said, his smile gone now. "You must!"

I heard Mother's footsteps clicking down the stairs, and then she came into the room. She put her hand on Tikhon's shoulder and asked him whether he had liked his supper. Tikhon had time for only a quick nod before Mother rushed me out of the room and up the stairs.

Papa was very talkative all through supper. He told us about his work, and although he tried to make it sound interesting, even funny at times, I did not listen much.

"How sad Tikhon must feel," I suddenly heard myself say, "so lonely and abandoned."

"Nonsense," Papa said. "He gets good food and care, and as soon as it gets dark he and I will go for a walk and get some fresh air."

"I'll go with you, Papa," I said.

"No, you will help me with the dishes," Mother said quickly.

After I had finished the dishes, I was sent to bed. But I decided not to fall asleep and to sneak down to Tikhon later. I sat up and waited for my parents to go to bed. Then I tiptoed to the door leading to the hall and was surprised to find it locked! I had no choice but to go back to bed.

While Tikhon's harmonica sobbed in the distance, I pleaded with God: "Please, help Tikhon. *Please!*"

Chapter Fifteen

Next day was Monday, and Papa left for work right after breakfast. Around noon, when Mr. Keller was done with my lessons and had left, the doorbell rang. I peeked down from upstairs and saw a huge man in the doorway. He introduced himself to Mother: "Police."

I did not hear what the policeman said, but my knees began to tremble and I suppressed a scream. I saw Mother shake her head and say, "You are

welcome to look for yourself," as she stepped aside
and let the policeman into the hall.

Panic came over me. I dashed down to the basement and burst into Tikhon's room. He was sitting
at the table, bent over his German grammar. I put
my hand over his mouth and whispered, "Shhh!
quiet! No word!"

I grabbed him by the hand. "Come!" I whispered, pulling a bewildered Tikhon upstairs and
outside. I had no plan, no idea: I knew only it
would be of no use to run away. We would be
caught. The chicken coop at the end of our property crossed my mind. No. The policeman would
certainly look there. Paralyzed with fear, I stood
and surveyed our large grounds, hoping to see a
place where Tikhon could hide.

Tikhon bent down to my ear. "Danger?" he
asked.

I nodded. "Police!"

By the grip of Tikhon's hand I could feel he knew
something had to be done quickly.

"Dere," he said, and started toward the vegetable garden.

"No good," I said. The vegetable garden was flat and empty and seemed to offer no possibility to hide anything.

"Yes . . . good," Tikhon said.

He walked to the spot where he had dug a six-foot-long trench a few weeks before, to store potatoes over winter under layers of straw and dirt. While he shoved aside the straw, I began to understand. It was big enough for Tikhon to lie down in. He covered his face with his large red handkerchief, and I helped him to pull the straw back over him.

Then I hurried back to Tikhon's room and waited, all the time listening to what was going on upstairs. Doors were opened and closed. Sometimes I could hear Mother's voice, but could not make out a word. She spoke faster and with a higher pitch than usual.

Then I heard footsteps coming down the basement stairs. Stay calm, I told myself, stay calm. I sat down in front of the dollhouse and began to move the furniture, trying to give the impression I was playing.

"Ah, this is the little lady who climbed the Zobten," the policeman said.

Nobody had ever called me "little lady" before. I liked it, but his voice was too sugary. I didn't trust him.

"Well," the policeman said, coming closer, "was it nice on the Zobten?"

"Very," I answered without taking my eyes off the dollhouse.

"And your friend—what's his name—how did he like it?"

"Fine," I said.

"I guess you like him, little lady, don't you?"

"Very much," I answered, as I busily rearranged some of the furniture in the dollhouse.

The policeman moved a chair close to me, sat down and watched. I glanced at Mother standing in the doorway, her face flushed.

"Well," the policeman started again, "I guess you would not like any harm to come to Tikhon, would you?"

I shook my head.

"You see, that means we have to find him."

"What for?" I asked.

"To take him back to prison where he will be safe."

"Safe?" I asked angrily. "Safe in prison?"

The policeman's smile vanished and I felt terrible: everything seemed to go from bad to worse.

"Why is it safe in prison?" I wanted to know.

"Because nobody can shoot him down in prison," the policeman answered.

"Shoot him down! Why would anybody want to shoot Tikhon?"

"Well, there are reasons, little lady. For one thing, he broke out of prison—he is a fugitive. Furthermore, he does not have any papers."

"But he is a good person," I said. "Mother says so herself."

The policeman smiled again, but I didn't trust his smile.

"Anybody who shoots Tikhon is a murderer," I declared, looking him straight in the face.

"The law is the law," the policeman answered, his smile gone. "Besides, it might not be necessary to shoot him if you are willing to help us find him."

"How can I?" I said. "I'm sure he is no longer on the face of this earth." There it was: a statement I could swear to without lying because Tikhon was *under* the earth.

"You have searched the whole house," I said, now feeling more daring. "Why don't you go outside and look? There are chicken coops and bushes and trees at the end of our property."

"I think I will," said the policeman, and he went outside, led by Mother.

I watched them from the basement window. The policeman didn't pay any attention to the fenced-in vegetable garden. He walked straight to the chicken coop and then disappeared in the bushes and trees. He must have searched very thoroughly, because it took a long time before he and Mother came into sight again.

Finally they returned to the house and the policeman seemed ready to leave. "I might have to ask you and your daughter to come to the station next week" were his parting words to Mother.

The moment the policeman drove off, I ran out to the vegetable garden.

"You are safe, Tikhon, safe!" I cried. Tikhon sat up and pulled his handkerchief from his face.

He got to his feet and shook off the dirt and straw. Together we walked back to his room and sat down across from each other. Neither of us said a word; we just sat and looked at each other, until the door opened and Mother appeared with a tray of hot tea and biscuits.

"You need this, Tikhon," she said.

Tikhon reached for Mother's hand, kissed it and then pressed his forehead against it. "Tanks," he murmured, "tanks, tanks, tanks."

Lying in bed that night, I took the harmonica music drifting into my dreams as something very special. Something I could have lost again, but still had. A treasure! And I looked forward to waking up to it the next morning.

But next morning there was no harmonica music. All was silent. I dressed quickly and went down to the basement. I knocked on Tikhon's door. No answer. I knocked again and waited. Finally I opened

106

the door. No Tikhon! The room was empty. But on the table I found a note.

In large, awkward letters it said:

I MUST GO. I BURDEN TO
YOU ALL. I FULL OF THANK
TO YOU. I WILL WRITE AFTER
I HOME. WILL TAKE LONG TIME.
TIKHON

I looked around. His Bible and his German grammar, the icon and the photo, all were gone. He had left the sketchbook behind, but it was the photo of little Tikhon sitting with his father in the beautiful sleigh which I longed to have more than anything.

Beside myself, I rushed upstairs and found Mother at her writing desk.

"He's gone!" Shoving Tikhon's note into her hand, I burst out crying.

"Don't cry, darling," Mother said. "Somehow Tikhon will make his way home, I know. And that will be the best for him."

Chapter Sixteen

A year passed. We did not hear from Tikhon. Twice the police had come to inquire whether we had had any contact with Tikhon, but then they stopped coming.

It was November again, and one late afternoon when I saw the top of the Zobten covered with the first snow of the season, I went to the basement. I got out my sled and sat down on it, fixing my eyes on the mountain. And while the Zobten's white cap slowly turned to orange, the sled began to glide. *Whish . . . whoosh . . . now we are starting our downhill ride. Hold on tight to Tikhon's back and pull up your legs. Pull your scarf tight over chin and nose! The faster we go, the colder it gets. The trees along the path stop being trees. They pull together into a blurry wall. Faster and faster the sled flies and Tikhon puts one foot on the ground. The snow crunches and creaks under his heavy boot, and the sled slows down. My cheeks prickle and burn with cold, but my heart is warm. Tikhon greets every rock flashing by and every curve with a joyous howl followed by laughter. He is in complete control of the sled and its speed, and though the ride is full of danger, I feel safe. I press my cheek against Tikhon's back and join in his joy and his laughter.*

Suddenly Mother's voice stops the ride.

"Inge, where are you?"

Tikhon was gone. The sled was still.

"Come here. The postman brought a package for you," I heard Mother saying.

A huge box with large colorful stamps and tags of many sizes sat on the kitchen table.

"For me?" I asked, astonished.

"Yes," Mother said, smiling. "Can you see where it's from?"

I shook my head no.

"Russia," Mother said softly.

The Volga rushed into my head, making me so dizzy I had to sit down.

"Shall I open it for you?" Mother asked.

I nodded, unable to move. I watched her carefully remove the tags and undo the string. Then slowly I got up and began to gather every little bit Mother took off the package. I wanted to save it all.

It took me a long time, but finally I lifted the lid. My hands dove into a mass of wood shavings till I felt something hard. I pulled it out carefully. It was a tiny vanity table with ruffles hanging from its oval tabletop. My initials were carved into the delicately etched frame around the mirror. I handed it gently to Mother and dug for more. A four-poster bed came next, a chair and a dresser followed, all beautifully carved and painted a deep greenish blue. There was more: a pair of embroidered slip-

111

pers, two little fur rugs, tiny vases with dried flowers, and a birdcage with a little parrot in it. The last thing I unwrapped was a tiny wooden doll with the most beautiful painted face and blond hair down to her waist. All the parts of her limbs could be bent into any position. She could sit on the pretty blue-green chair if I wanted her to. As in a dream I kept picking up each piece of furniture again and again, studying it in detail.

"Inge, here is something you overlooked," Mother said, handing me a blue envelope with my name printed on it in large letters.

Slowly I opened the envelope. It was the photo of little Tikhon, sitting beside his father in the sleigh. He was looking straight at me; we were eye to eye, partners in crime and joy, and neither miles nor years seemed to separate us. We were of one age and together again.